CANADA

Pennsylvania

New Jersey

Washington, D.C

Delaware

Maryland

Ohio

Kentucky

Virginia

North Carolina

Tennessee

South Carolina

Georgia

Alabama

Florida

ATLANTIC OCEAN

N

GULF OF MEXICO

Your

Best Friend, Kate

by Pat Brisson

illustrations by Rick Brown

Aladdin Books
Macmillan Publishing Company   New York
Maxwell Macmillan Canada   Toronto
Maxwell Macmillan International
New York   Oxford   Singapore   Sydney

First Aladdin Books edition 1992
Text copyright © 1989 by Pat Brisson

Illustrations copyright © 1989 by Rick Brown

Aladdin Books
Macmillan Publishing Company
866 Third Avenue
New York, NY 10022

Maxwell Macmillan Canada, Inc.
1200 Eglinton Avenue East
Suite 200
Don Mills, Ontario M3C 3N1

Macmillan Publishing Company is part of the Maxwell
Communication Group of Companies

Printed and bound in Hong Kong by
South China Printing Company (1988) Ltd.

A hardcover edition of *Your Best Friend, Kate* is available from
Bradbury Press, an affiliate of Macmillan, Inc.

10   9   8   7   6   5   4   3   2   1

Library of Congress Cataloging-in-Publication Data
Brisson, Pat.
Your best friend, Kate / by Pat Brisson; illustrations by Rick
Brown.—1st Aladdin Books ed.
p.   cm.
Summary: Kate's letters to her best friend back home chart her
family's trip through the South and back up through Kentucky, Ohio,
and Pennsylvania, and reveal her true affection for her brother with
whom she is always fighting.
ISBN 0-689-71545-5
[1. United States—Description and travel—Fiction. 2. Travel—
Fiction. 3. Brothers and sisters—Fiction. 4. Letters.]
I. Brown, Rick, 1946-   ill. II. Title.
PZ7.B78046Yo   1992
[E]—dc20   91-15245   CIP   AC

For my mother, Jane Gerity McDonough,
in memory of my father, Thomas F. McDonough,
and for brothers and sisters everywhere,
especially mine

— P.B.

To Jerome and Jennie
— R.B.

Dear Lucy,

I am leaving this note taped to your door because we are leaving and it is only 6 o'clock. My mother said even best friends don't wake each other up at this hour of the morning. I know you will take good care of Buster and Bruno. They are waiting for you on the shelf in the garage. They need to have their bowl cleaned twice a week, and if you sing "God Bless America" to them while you're scrubbing, I know they will appreciate it.

My mother says the next four weeks will fly by and we'll be back in New Jersey before I know it. She's only saying that because she doesn't have to share the backseat with Brian. I'll write you often if I survive him.

Your best friend,
Kate

state flower
BLACK-EYED SUSAN

July 9, Maryland

Dear Lucy,

How is everything in New Jersey? Baltimore is nice. Today we went to the National Aquarium. We saw a zillion fish and three beluga whales! Belugas can live for a long time—some of them for over thirty years. That's almost as old as my father! The aquarium made me a little homesick for Buster and Bruno. Tell them I said hello. Brian said it was too bad we hadn't brought them along—some of the sharks looked hungry. (He thinks he's so funny.)

Your best friend,
Kate

BALTIMORE ORIOLE
State Bird

BELUGA WHALE

July 12, District of Columbia

Dear Lucy,

    Washington, D.C., is great! So far, we've been to the Lincoln Memorial, the Washington Monument, the National Gallery of Art, and the White House (but we didn't see the president). Today we went to the National Air and Space Museum. Brian told me I should be an astronaut when I grow up because I look like something from outer space and maybe I could find my true family out there somewhere. I told him that any space creature would make a better little brother and would probably be smarter and nicer looking, too. My father said if we didn't stop fighting with each other he'd send us both to the moon, but I don't think he really meant it.

                          Your best friend,
                          Kate

Sculpture at Museum of Art

State Flower Dogwood

State Bird Cardinal

State Tree Longleaf Pine

July 14, North Carolina

Dear Lucy,

I think we visited every Civil War site and restored cotton plantation from Richmond, Virginia, to Raleigh, North Carolina. We keep changing centuries, and I can't decide which I like best—the 18th, 19th, or 20th.

My favorite plantation in Virginia is called, get this, Shirley. It has a three-story-high staircase that seems to stay up by magic—I couldn't see anything supporting it! Our guide told us it's the only one of its kind in the whole country.

Brian is driving me crazy with all this Civil War stuff. He's even divided the backseat into the North and South and says if I cross the line it will mean just one thing—WAR!

Your best friend,
Kate

State
Flower
Carolina
Jessamine
←

July 17, South Carolina

Dear Lucy,

We went on a house and garden tour in Charleston today. One garden has a pretty little goldfish pond with lily pads and five fat goldfish in it. I asked my father if we could build a pond in the backyard for Buster and Bruno. Brian said, "A goldfish pond? That's dumb! Why don't we build something useful like a skateboard ramp?" Isn't that typical?

Anyway, the house tour was interesting. I think one house has a ghost—I could just feel it in my bones.

At another place, called Magnolia Gardens, we rented bikes and rode on the bike paths and had a picnic lunch. And you should have seen the miniature horses—they didn't even come up to my waist!

Your best friend,
Kate

Carolina
Wren
State
Bird
←

State
Flower
Cherokee
Rose

July 18, Georgia

Dear Lucy,

The temperature hit 103° today while we were
visiting old Fort Jackson in Savannah, and the cannon
I touched was so hot I nearly burned my hand. My
mother said we would all melt into puddles if we
didn't find some way to cool off, so we ended up
getting ice-cream cones and going to the beach.
Brian took my picture by the lighthouse. (I hope
he didn't cut off my head.) I took a picture of him
doing a handstand in the water, but of course all
you can see are his feet . . . his best feature.

Your best friend,
Kate

Brown
Thrasher
State
Bird

← Anhinga

State Flower Orange Blossom

July 22, Florida

Dear Lucy,

Greetings from the land of palm trees and pink flamingos! We're staying at Aunt Ginny and Uncle Bill's house in Tallahassee for a few days. Yesterday we went to Wakulla Springs and rode in a glass-bottom boat. I saw three alligators! We also saw a big black bird called an anhinga that swims underwater to catch fish.

When Brian found out that some of the old Tarzan movies were made here, he thumped his chest and practiced his Tarzan yell.

"Me, Tarzan—you, Jane," he said, poking me with his finger.

"You've got it all wrong," I told him. "I'm Kate, and you're *crazy!*"

Your best friend,
Kate

State Tree Sabal Palmetto

state bird Mockingbird

Cajun
Red
Fish

Dixie

State
Flower
Camellia

State Bird
Yellowhammer

State
tree
Longleaf
Pine

July 24, Alabama

Dear Lucy,

We went to a big antique show at the Montgomery Civic Center today. I saw the most beautiful bowl for Buster and Bruno, all carved with birds and apple blossoms. But my mother said there was no way she would buy an antique punch bowl—that once belonged to Millard Fillmore's grandmother—for fish to swim in. I offered to take Buster and Bruno out whenever she wanted to use the punch bowl, but she said, "Katherine Marie, that is *not* one of your better ideas."

In the end, we bought a picture called *Along the Alabama* that has people in old-fashioned clothes riding in a boat on the Alabama River. My father said it would remind us of the ride we took on a riverboat here, and called it a suitable souvenir.

Your best friend,
Kate

P.S. We drove into the central time zone yesterday. We had to set our watches back one hour!

State Flower IRIS →

State Bird Mockingbird ↓

July 26, Tennessee

Dear Lucy,

Of all the cities we've been in so far, I like the sound of this one best—Chattanooga. However, my father whistles "Chattanooga Choo Choo" every time he sees it on a sign. Finally, my mother said, "Henry, please!" which really meant that if he didn't stop whistling that same tune over and over again she would go crazy.

We went to some caverns on Lookout Mountain and saw stalactites and stalagmites with names like "The Candlestick and the Cactus" and "Steak and Potatoes." It was pretty eerie being in such a big cave. Brian said it would be a great place to have a Halloween party. For once, I had to admit he had a good idea.

Your best friend,
Kate

P.S. We're back on eastern standard time!

↑ **State tree Tulip Poplar**

July 28, Kentucky

Dear Lucy,

    You would love Lexington—there are horses everywhere! Today we went to the Kentucky Horse Park and visited the International Museum of the Horse. We saw silver trophies and beautifully painted horse-drawn sleighs. During the Parade of Breeds, they brought out all different kinds of horses—Arabian, Welsh pony, Tennessee walker. . . . My favorite was the American painted pony, which looks like it has polka dots.

    But best of all, Brian and I went on a trail ride with a bunch of other kids. (Brian needed help getting on his horse but I didn't.)

    Later, in the Hall of Champions, we met John Henry, a Thoroughbred who has won 6½ million dollars in races. When he looked at me with his big brown eyes, I said, "I think I'm in love!" Brian said, "That's good, Kate, because you've got a face only a horse could love."

    The things I have to put up with!

Your best friend,
Kate

State Flower Goldenrod

Kentucky ↗ Coffee tree State tree

State Bird
Cardinal

OHIO
STATE
HOUSE

State
Bird
Cardinal

State Tree
Buckeye

July 30, Ohio

Dear Lucy,

My father took us to see Ohio State University in Columbus because he went to school there in the old days. Brian and I got OHIO BUCKEYES T-shirts. Brian said, "Kate's T-shirt should say BUCKTEETH instead of BUCKEYES."

So I said, "You'd better watch out or you'll have BLACK EYES to go with your BUCKEYES," which I thought was pretty fast thinking, but my father didn't agree.

Your best friend,
Kate

State
Flower
Scarlet
Carnation

State Tree
HEMLOCK

July 31, Pennsylvania

Dear Lucy,

The Allegheny and Monongahela rivers join here in Pittsburgh to form the Ohio River. Brian liked the name Monongahela so much that he kept repeating it over and over like a chant: Mononga*he*la, Mononga*he*la, all the way up Mount Washington on the incline trolley to view where the rivers join; Mononga*he*la, Mononga*he*la, the whole time we were at the zoo.

But when he began to sing Mononga*he*la, Mononga*he*la, to the tune of "Three Blind Mice," my father made a deal with him. He said if Brian would stop with the Mononga*he*las, we could all go to see the Pirates play at Three Rivers Stadium. Brian agreed. I'm glad—you know how much I *love* baseball.

Your best friend,
Kate

State Flower
Mountain
Laurel

State Bird
Ruffed
Grouse

August 3, Pennsylvania

Dear Lucy,

    I love being at my Great Aunt Mag's house in Lancaster. But when I saw the picture of Buster and Bruno and me, on the refrigerator, I realized how much I missed them. (And you, of course.) I went to the store and bought some fish food, and Aunt Mag gave me an old crystal shaker to put it in. It looked absolutely elegant, and I knew Buster and Bruno would love it.

    Unfortunately, my father thought it was some kind of special seasoning and sprinkled it all over his roast beef sandwich. He had already eaten half of it when I noticed him reaching for the shaker again and asked him to please not use too much or there wouldn't be any left for Buster and Bruno.

    He said, "What are you talking about, Kate?"

    When I explained how I'd put fish food in the shaker, he decided not to eat any more lunch, and Brian and I got to split his dessert.

Your best friend,
Kate

August 4, Pennsylvania

Dear Lucy,

    We're leaving for home tomorrow. I can't wait to see you and Buster and Bruno. When I get my pictures developed, I can show you all the great places we've seen.

    Brian is going to stay here with Aunt Mag for two weeks, and then she's going to drive out with him. Brian said, "Two weeks without Kate—now that's a *real* vacation!"

    I said, "You'll miss me before I'm even gone one day."

    "Never!" he said.

    "Just you wait," I told him.

    My father told Aunt Mag that more people should take vacations like this to see the country and bring their families closer together and that maybe next year we'd take a trip out West. My mother said he was either very brave or very foolish.

Your best friend,
Kate

Dear Brian,

    I'm leaving this note on your pillow because I know how homesick you'll be the first night away from us. Last year when I stayed at Aunt Mag's, I tried to pretend I wasn't homesick, but Aunt Mag figured it out and made a big batch of oatmeal raisin cookies and said I could have one whenever I missed home. I already told her your favorites are chocolate chip.

    I promise I won't touch any of your stuff while you're away, except maybe that new video game you got for your birthday—nobody's perfect.

Your favorite sister,
Kate

CANADA
Pennsylvania
New Jersey
Washington, D.C
Delaware
Maryland
Ohio
Kentucky
Virginia
North Carolina
South Carolina
Tennessee
Georgia
Alabama
Florida
ATLANTIC OCEAN
GULF OF MEXICO
N